Where Does the Sky End, Grandpa?

MARTHA ALEXANDER

HARCOURT BRACE & COMPANY

SAN DIEGO NEW YORK LONDON

Library of Congress Cataloging-in-Publication Data
Alexander, Martha G.
Where does the sky end, Grandpa?/by Martha Alexander. — 1st ed.
p. cm.
Summary: A grandfather and child
take a walk outdoors, admiring such
natural wonders as the endless sky, flowing stream,
and seeds blowing in the wind.
ISBN 0-15-295603-4
[1. Nature — Fiction. 2. Grandfathers — Fiction.] I. Title.
PZ7.A3777Whr 1992
[E] — dc20 90-36793

B C D E F

Printed in Singapore

The illustrations in this book were done in
Winsor and Newton watercolors, Conté pastels, and Derwent colored
pencils on d'Arches hot-press watercolor paper.

The display type and text type were set in
Goudy Old Style by Thompson Type, San Diego, California.

Color separations were made by Bright Arts, Ltd., Singapore.
Printed and bound by Tien Wah Press, Singapore

Production supervision by Warren Wallerstein and Cheryl Kennedy
Designed by Trina Stahl

For Kim and Allen
and their children
and their children's children,
with love

Where does the sky end, Grandpa?

It doesn't end, little one.
It goes on and on forever.

But Grandpa, where is forever?

Come, little one, let's go look.
First let's climb to the top of this tree.

Oh, Grandpa, I can see a long way.
I can see cows and sheep and ducks
on a pond, and I can see a river and a covered
bridge. I can see big snowy mountains
and a bird flying high in the sky.

Grandpa, do you think that bird can fly to forever?

Maybe, little one — maybe it can.

Look, Grandpa, there's a fish jumping
in the stream and a frog on a rock.
There's a floating leaf that
looks like a ship. Where does the stream
come from, Grandpa?

Snow melts in the mountains, little one,
and rain comes from the sky. The water
flows into low places and makes streams.

And where is the stream going, Grandpa?

Streams flow into rivers and rivers flow to the sea.

Let's go, Grandpa, let's go to the sea.

The sea is very far away, little one.
It is too far to walk.

Does the sea go on forever, Grandpa?

Oh, no, little one, there is land on the other side of the sea.

Then let's find more of forever, Grandpa.
Where else can we look?

Look all around you, little one—what do you see?

Why, Grandpa, I see flowers everywhere.
They go up over the hill and touch the sky.

This flower is dried and covered with seeds.

Blow it, little one, and see what happens.

The seeds are flying in the wind, Grandpa. Look! They're going far, far away — maybe to forever!

Wherever a seed lands, little one, a new flower will grow.

Even across the sea, Grandpa?

Yes, little one, even across the sea.

The sun is going down, Grandpa.
But it will come back, won't it?

Yes, little one, it always comes back.

Look, Grandpa, look! There's the moon.
It's so big and round!

And look, little one, the very first star.
You can make a wish.

Can I wish for anything I want, Grandpa?

Yes, little one, anything you want.

Then, Grandpa, I wish I'd grow wings
like a bird.

I'd flap my wings and fly with the wind . . .

. . . and blow the seeds across the sea.

Then I would fly up to the sky . . .

. . . and float on a cloud. I'd look down and
see the snowy mountains and the streams
and the rivers going to the sea.
I'd see places I've never, ever seen.
I'd see far away — maybe to forever!

Then I'd put a flower on the moon.

I'd catch two stars and bring them back—
one for you and one for me.

Grandpa, did you make a wish?

Yes, little one, I did. I wished that your wish would come true.